With special thanks to Anne Marie Ryan
For Jane Powell, who is a star

ORCHARD BOOKS

First published in Great Britain in 2017 by The Watts Publishing Group

1 3 5 7 9 10 8 6 4 2

Text copyright © Hothouse Fiction, 2017
Illustrations copyright © Orchard Books, 2017

The moral rights of the author and illustrator have been asserted.

A CIP catalogue record for this book
is available from the British Library.

ISBN 978 1 40835 097 3

Printed and bound in Great Britain by Clays Ltd, St Ives plc

The paper and board used in this book are made from wood from responsible sources.

Orchard Books
An imprint of
Hachette Children's Group
Part of The Watts Publishing Group Limited
Carmelite House
50 Victoria Embankment
London EC4Y 0DZ

An Hachette UK Company
www.hachette.co.uk
www.hachettechildrens.co.uk

Series created by Hothouse Fiction
www.hothousefiction.com

Star Science

ROSIE BANKS

Wishing Star Palace

The Secret Princess Promise

"I promise that I will be kind and brave,

Using my magic to help and save,

Granting wishes and doing my best,

To make people smile and bring happiness."

☽ CONTENTS ☾

CHAPTER ONE
Moon Mystery

"Don't let go!" cried Elsie, Mia Thompson's little sister.

"I won't," panted Mia, holding on to the back of Elsie's pink bike and running to keep up as her sister pedalled. "You're doing great!"

DING! DING!

Elsie rang her bicycle bell again proudly.

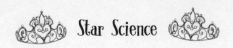

Their mum looked up from the magazine she was reading on a nearby bench and gave them a thumbs-up.

They had been in the park all afternoon, teaching Elsie how to ride her bike without stabilisers. The sun was beginning to set, but Elsie still hadn't quite got the hang of it yet.

As they reached the end of the path, Elsie squeezed her brakes and the bike squealed to a stop.

"Well done," gasped Mia, clutching her side and trying to catch her breath. Teaching someone how to ride a bike was exhausting!

Elsie turned her bike around. "This time, I want to try all by myself," she said.

"OK," said Mia. "I'll start you off, then I'll let go. Ready?"

Elsie nodded determinedly and gripped the handlebars. As she started to pedal, Mia jogged along behind her, holding the back of the seat lightly. When they were halfway down the path, she let go.

For a few moments, Elsie cycled forward on her own. But then she glanced back at Mia for reassurance – and wobbled off to the side.

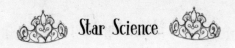

"Whoa!" wailed Elsie.

"Don't look at me," coached Mia. "Watch where you're going!"

It was too late. Elsie had lost her balance. The bike wobbled and then—

CRASH!

Elsie flew off the bike and sprawled on to the path. The bike lay on top of her, its wheels spinning wildly.

"Are you OK?" cried Mia, running over to her sister. She lifted the bike off Elsie and helped her sit up. Blood was blooming on Elsie's knee. "Does it hurt?"

Elsie nodded, her bottom lip wobbling.

"You poor thing, that looks nasty," said Mia, giving Elsie a big hug.

Mia could
tell that her
little sister was
trying to fight
back tears, but
one escaped and
fell on to Mia's
shoulder with
a plop.

"I'm never
going to learn how to ride a bike on my
own," sobbed Elsie.

"Of course you will," Mia said, rubbing her
sister's back gently. "It took me ages to learn
how to ride a bike, too."

"Really?" asked Elsie, sniffling.

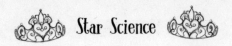

"Yup," confirmed Mia. "Charlotte learned how to ride without stabilisers way before me. But then, she's good at anything sporty." Charlotte Williams was Mia's best friend in the whole world. The summer Mia had learned how to ride a bike, the two of them had spent hours cycling around the park together. A while back, Charlotte's family had moved to California, but the girls still saw each other – because they shared a magical secret!

"Is my bike OK?" asked Elsie, interrupting Mia's thoughts.

Mia propped the bike against a tree and inspected it for damage. It was decorated with pictures of princesses and had pink and

purple tassels dangling from the handlebars.
There was even a white basket with plastic
daisies attached to the front.

"It's fine," said Mia.

"Phew," said Elsie. "I'm glad the princesses
didn't get scratched." She sighed longingly.
"I wish I was a princess. Then I could wear
a beautiful tiara instead of a boring old bike
helmet."

Mia laughed. "Even princesses wear
helmets when they go cycling."

Elsie shook her head emphatically. "No,
princesses don't ride bikes. They just dance
at fancy balls and wear sparkly tiaras."

Mia thought about the princesses she
knew. Though they did like dancing at balls

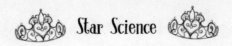

and wearing tiaras, they also did lots of other cool things – like swimming, painting and horse riding. They had jobs too – one was a vet, another was a teacher, and there was even a pop star princess! Of course she couldn't tell Elsie any of this, because Mia's princess friends were Secret Princesses! They kept the fact that they could grant wishes using magic a secret. They only wore their tiaras when they visited Wishing Star Palace, a magical place hidden in the clouds. The only reason Mia knew any of this was because she and Charlotte were training to become Secret Princesses too!

"Let's get you cleaned up," said Mia, helping Elsie to her feet.

As they wheeled their bikes back to where their mum was sitting, Elsie pointed up at the sky. "Look, Mia."

A full moon was peeking out from behind pink clouds as the afternoon turned into twilight.

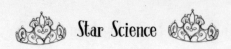

"The moon is so pretty tonight," said Mia.

"Is it really made of cheese?" Elsie asked curiously.

"No," said Mia, with a giggle. "I think it's made of rock."

"What type of rock?" asked Elsie.

"I'm not sure," said Mia. "But we can look it up on the computer when we get home."

Thinking about the moon reminded Mia of the four moonstones she and Charlotte needed to earn for the next stage of their training. Mia couldn't wait to get started – it felt like ages since she'd seen Charlotte. Looking down at the necklace she always wore, Mia's heart leapt. The half-heart pendant was glowing!

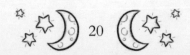

"Oh dear," Mum said, catching sight of Elsie's skinned knee as they approached. Rummaging in her handbag, Mum dug out a tissue and  a plaster. She dabbed away the blood and stuck the plaster on Elsie's knee.

"There!" she said. "As good as new!"

Elsie smiled back bravely.

Tucking her magazine into her handbag, Mum stood up and said, "It's going to be dark soon. Why don't we let Mia have a quick bike ride, and I'll help you, Elsie."

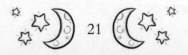

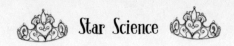
"Thanks, Mum!" Mia said.

She got on to her bike, which was the exact same shade of blue as her eyes. Mia pedalled off as fast as she could go, her long blonde hair streaming out behind her. When she was sure that she was out of sight, Mia stopped and rested her bike against a tree.

Ducking behind the tree, Mia grasped her glowing necklace. "I wish I could be with Charlotte," she said.

The light shining out of the pendant grew brighter and brighter. It swirled around Mia, until she was surrounded by a sparkly magical glow. She wasn't worried about leaving her bike behind – no time would pass at home while she was having an adventure.

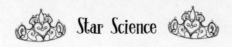

Mia's feet, now sporting sparkling ruby slippers, landed on the grass outside Wishing Star Palace at dusk. Touching her head, Mia realised that her bike helmet had been replaced with the diamond tiara she always wore at the palace. Her clothes, too, had been magically transformed into a beautiful gold dress.

Nearby, a girl with curly brown hair was staring at the palace. Like Mia, she was wearing a tiara and ruby slippers, but her dress was the same shade of pink as the roses climbing up the palace's white walls. She hadn't noticed Mia arrive.

"Charlotte!" Mia cried, running over to greet her best friend.

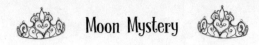
"Hi, Mia," said Charlotte, hugging her tight.

"What are you looking at?" Mia asked.

"The astronomy tower," said Charlotte, pointing up at the one of the palace's four turrets. It had a bright light shining from its windows. "I think there's something happening up there!"

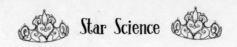

"I wonder what's going on?" said Mia, squinting at the astronomy tower.

"There's only one way to find out," said Charlotte. "Come on!"

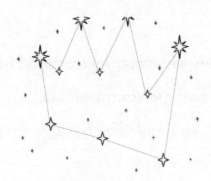

CHAPTER TWO
Tiara in the Sky

As Charlotte and Mia linked arms and headed towards the palace, a familiar voice called out, "Hey! Wait up!"

Mia turned and saw the famous pop star, Alice de Silver. Instead of the trendy mini skirts, glittery tops and high-heeled boots she wore on stage, the singer was wearing a scarlet dress and a gold necklace with a

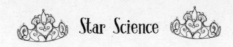

musical note pendant. There was a tiara resting on her strawberry-blonde hair.

"Alice!" Mia and Charlotte shouted, running over to embrace her.

They weren't just Alice de Silver's biggest fans – they were also her friends! Alice had been their babysitter when they were little, long before she had won a TV talent contest and become a huge pop star. It was because of Alice that they were training to become Secret Princesses, just like her. She had spotted their potential and given them magic wish necklaces before Charlotte had moved to California.

"I'll just let Princess Luna know that we're on our way," said Princess Alice, happily.

She held her moonstone bracelet to her lips. "Hi, everyone, it's me – Alice," she said, speaking into the pearly white gem. "I've just arrived at the palace. Mia and Charlotte are here too."

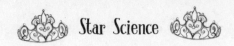

Charlotte grinned. "That bracelet is so cool – and useful."

"I really wish we had one," said Mia longingly. "We could talk all the time!"

"Soon," said Alice, ruffling their hair affectionately.

"You'll get your moonstone bracelets once you've completed the next stage of your training."

"Maybe we can start today!" Charlotte said, jigging about on the spot. "And earn our first moonstone!"

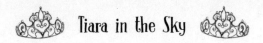

The mention of moonstones made Mia glance up at the astronomy tower again. "Do you know why we've been called here?" she asked nervously. "Is Princess Poison causing trouble again?"

Princess Poison was the Secret Princesses' enemy. Instead of granting wishes, she spoiled them. Whereas Secret Princesses were kind, loyal and brave, Princess Poison was cruel and spiteful. It was hard for Mia to believe, but Princess Poison had once been a Secret Princess. She'd been banished from Wishing Star Palace for using her magic to get more power, and since then she'd been determined to stop the Secret Princesses and spoil wishes.

"I don't think so," said Alice. "Luna asked us all to come here – she said that she had some exciting news."

"Oh, goodie," said Charlotte, rubbing her hands together in anticipation. "I wonder what it could be?"

"What are we waiting for?" said Alice, lifting up the hem of her dress to reveal her sparkling ruby slippers. "Let's go!"

They all clicked the heels of their ruby slippers together three times. "The Astronomy Tower!" they cried in unison.

WHOOSH! Their magical slippers whisked them to the top of the Astronomy Tower, which was full of Secret Princesses chatting happily. A gold telescope was

pointed out of the window, at the night sky.

Mia suddenly remembered the question her sister had asked about the moon. She still didn't know the answer – but she knew someone who would.

"Hi, Luna," Mia said to a princess with short, dark hair and a necklace with a moon pendant. "What type of rock is the moon made from?"

"It's actually made from two different types of rock," said Luna, smiling kindly at Mia. "They're called basalt and anorthosite." Back in the real world, Princess Luna was a scientist who was training to become an astronaut. She knew practically everything about the stars and planets!

"Thanks," said Mia, hoping she could remember those names for Elsie.

"Would you like a biscuit?" offered a princess with cherry-red hair and a pendant shaped like a cupcake. Princess Sylvie, who owned a bakery in the real world, held out an empty plate.

"Er, OK," said Charlotte, looking at the plate in confusion.

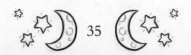

Sylvie waved her wand and two star-shaped biscuits whizzed over and landed on the plate. "Ta da!"

"Mmm!" said Mia, biting into the biscuit. A fizzy sensation filled her mouth as she chewed – the biscuits had popping candy in them!

"These are amazing," said Charlotte, crunching happily.

"I call them Shooting Star biscuits," said Sylvie, beaming.

"Ahem!" said Princess Luna, tapping her wand against a glass.

The chattering princesses fell silent and looked at Luna expectantly.

"Thank you all so much for coming tonight," Luna said. "I have some very exciting news – the Tiara Constellation has appeared in the sky!"

"Oooh!" Excited murmurs filled the astronomy tower.

Charlotte turned to Mia, a questioning look on her face. Mia shrugged. She'd never heard of the Tiara Constellation, either.

"What's the Tiara Constellation?" Charlotte asked.

"It's a special group of stars shaped just like a tiara," explained Luna. "It isn't visible very often, which is why it's so exciting.

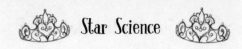
Come and have a look," she said, beckoning them over to the telescope.

Mia put her eye to the lens but she only saw black.

"I'll adjust it for you," said Luna, fiddling with some knobs and dials.

"Oh my gosh!" gasped Mia, as stars suddenly came into focus, sparkling like

diamonds against the
black night sky. The
tiara had four points,
and the stars at the tip
of each point shone more
brightly than the others.

"Look, Charlotte," Mia said, stepping away
so her friend could see.

"That's amazing!" said Charlotte, peering
through the telescope.

"The four stars at the tips of the tiara are
powerfully magical," said Luna. "I'm going
to grant the first wish made on each of those
stars. The magic from those wishes will keep
the palace hidden in the clouds until the
next time the tiara constellation appears."

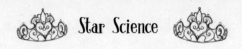

"That's why it's called Wishing Star Palace," said Alice.

"Wow," said Charlotte. "I always wondered about the name."

"Can I have another look?" asked Mia. She put her eye to the lens. One star was so dazzling she had to look away. "That's odd," she said, blinking. "One of the stars is even brighter than it was a minute ago."

Luna looked through the telescope. "You're right," she said, her grin nearly as bright as the star. "Someone must have made a wish on it!"

A hush fell over the princesses as Luna pointed her wand high up at the sky and called out:

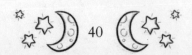

Twinkle, twinkle,
tiara so bright,
Four shining stars of
magical light.
Grant someone's dearest
wish tonight,
And keep the palace
hidden from sight.

As she waved her wand
to complete the spell, a
strange green mist rolled
across the sky. It was so thick

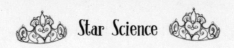

that it completely blocked out the tiara constellation.

"What's going on?" Charlotte asked.

"Where did the stars go?" Mia said.

"I'm not sure," said Luna. "I'd better check my equipment." She went over to a big computer. A message began scrolling down the computer screen:

Twinkle, twinkle, tiara so bright,
I will spoil a wish tonight.
To stop me you'll have to be clever,
Or Luna's magic will be lost for ever!

"Oh no!" cried Mia in dismay. "What's Princess Poison done now?"

CHAPTER THREE
Science Day

"I've got to clear the mist," said Princess Luna, waving her wand. A few green sparks shot from her wand and fizzled to the ground. She shook her wand and tried again – but it still didn't work.

"That's odd," said Luna. She turned to face the other Secret Princesses, and they all gasped when they saw her.

"What?" asked Luna. "What's wrong?"

"It's your tiara," said Mia, pointing.

"And your necklace," said Charlotte.

"They're green!" exclaimed Alice.

Luna's tiara, necklace and wand had turned the same dark green as the mist in the sky. Her bracelet and ring were green, too. The jewelled slippers on her feet still glittered, but now they

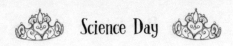

looked like emeralds instead of rubies.

"See if your shoes work," suggested Princess Sylvie. "Try going to the kitchen."

Luna clicked her heels together three times. "The kitchen!" she called. But nothing happened.

"The green mist must be cursed," said Alice. "It's stopped your magic from working."

The other princesses tried to clear the mist. Their wands fired magic into the sky, but Princess Poison's curse was too powerful – the thick green mist still blocked the tiara constellation from view.

"Someone has already made a wish on the first tiara star," said Luna, looking anxious.

"How can I grant it if my magic isn't working?"

That's why Luna is a Secret Princess, thought Mia. Luna was more concerned about the person she wanted to help than about what Princess Poison had done to her.

"We'll grant the tiara star wishes," offered Charlotte.

"We'd love to," said Mia, thinking of the four moonstones they needed to earn. "It will help us pass the next stage of our training."

"That's a great idea," said Alice. "Granting the tiara star wishes is the only way to break Princess Poison's curse."

"You'll need to be very careful," Luna warned them. "Princess Poison knows that if

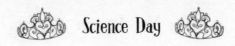

we don't grant the tiara star wishes, Wishing
Star Palace won't be hidden any more."

"She'll do everything she can to stop
you," said Princess Sylvie.

"Don't worry," said Charlotte, putting her
arm around Mia's shoulder. "There are two of
us and only one of her."

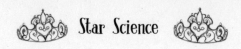

"Should we go to the Mirror Room?" asked Mia. In another of the palace's towers, there was a magic mirror that showed whose wish needed granting.

"You don't need to," said Luna. "Use the telescope – it's magic."

Mia peered into the telescope. Words suddenly appeared on the glass. She read them out loud:

Grant a wish on a magical star,
Make someone happy,
wherever they are.
Earn four stones, as pale as the moon,
And you will get your bracelet soon!

The sparkling words
vanished and were
replaced with an
image of a girl
with long, wavy
brown hair. She
was biting her
nails nervously.

"Oh dear," Mia said,
stepping away from the telescope so
Charlotte could see. "The girl we need to
help doesn't seem very happy. I wonder
what's wrong?"

As Charlotte gazed through the telescope,
she said, "There are more words."

"What do they say?" asked Mia.

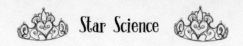

Charlotte read the message in her clear, confident voice:

Touch the telescope to see a star,
Call Tilly's name and you'll go far.

Mia and Charlotte both gripped the telescope. Then Charlotte said, "Ready? One, two, three—"

"Tilly!" they both cried at the same time.

Just as the message had promised, magic swept them far away from the palace. A galaxy of twinkling stars whizzed past them and they landed in a school hall, filled with boys and girls sitting cross-legged on the wooden floor. Thanks to the magic, none

of the children or teachers noticed Mia and Charlotte appear out of thin air. Mia and Charlotte's princess outfits had magically transformed into normal clothes, which helped them blend in with the pupils.

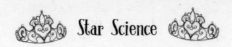

"They're so lucky," whispered Mia. "They don't have to wear a school uniform."

"Shh!" said a boy sitting next to them. "Mrs Cooper is about to begin the assembly. You don't want the headmistress to catch you talking."

Mia and Charlotte turned their attention to a lady in a grey skirt and smart jacket.

"Welcome to Science Day," said Mrs Cooper, smiling at the children. "We're going to spend all day doing experiments. Things might get a bit messy!"

The children giggled. All except one – the girl from the telescope!

Mia nudged Charlotte and pointed at Tilly discreetly, not wanting to get told off

for whispering. Unlike her classmates, Tilly didn't seem very excited at the thought of a day doing science experiments. In fact, she looked absolutely miserable!

"Each class has been working very hard on science projects this term," continued the headteacher. "You'll be testing them out at the end of the day."

At this, Tilly looked even more glum.

"Now, to get Science Day started, Mr Watson is going to do an experiment," said the headteacher.

A jolly-looking teacher with a beard and a tweed jacket came to the front. With a flourish, the teacher took a mint out of his pocket and showed it to the children.

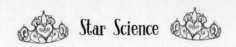

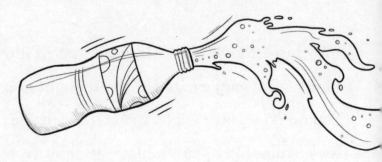

Unscrewing the lid on a big bottle of lemonade, he dropped the mint inside.

FIZZZZZZZZ!

A jet of bubbles spurted high in the air, nearly reaching the ceiling!

The children clapped and cheered.

"Cool!" shouted a girl with a polka-dotted bow in her red hair.

"Wicked!" whooped a girl wearing trendy hot pink trainers.

"The bubbles in lemonade are caused by a gas called carbon dioxide," Mr Watson

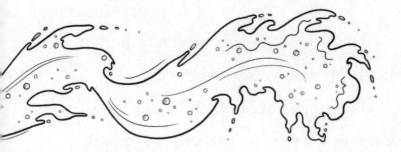

explained. "The mint makes bubbles form more quickly and shoot up like a fountain."

"It's time to get to work, everyone!" said the headteacher. "There are fun experiments to do in every classroom but please stay with your class."

"Remember," added Mr Watson, "the experiments you do today will count towards your end-of-term grade, so be sure to try and earn some gold stars!"

All around Mia and Charlotte, children were chatting excitedly.

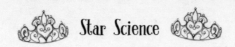

"That wasn't an experiment," Charlotte joked. "It was an experi-MINT!"

Mia grinned at her friend's pun, but she knew it was time for them to get to work, too. They needed to find out what Tilly's wish was.

"Come on," Mia said, scrambling to her feet. "We don't want to lose track of Tilly."

She needn't have worried – Tilly hadn't moved. She was still sitting on the floor, dejectedly picking at a plaster on her knee.

"Should we go and talk to her?" Mia asked. She always felt a bit awkward about approaching new people. Luckily, Charlotte was as confident as Mia was shy.

"Hey," said Charlotte, striding up to Tilly.

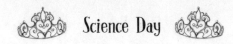

"Are you excited about Science Day?"

"Not really," said Tilly, slowly standing up and smoothing down her pretty denim dress. "Science is my worst subject."

"Don't you like doing experiments?" Mia asked, surprised.

Tilly shook her head sadly. "They always go wrong for me."

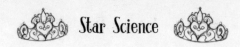

"Maybe Science Day will be more fun than you think," said Charlotte encouragingly.

"I hope so …" Tilly said. "My teacher, Miss Powell, says I have to improve my science grade or I won't be allowed to play

on the girls' football team any more. I wish I could get a good mark in science or I won't be able to play in the tournament this weekend."

Mia glanced over at Charlotte, who raised her eyebrow at her friend in reply. Now they knew

what was worrying Tilly – and what wish
they needed to grant!

"Do you want to do some experiments
with us?" asked Charlotte.

"Trust me," said Tilly. "You don't want to
work with me – I always mess it up."

"That's OK," said Mia. "We can help each
other out."

"I'm Charlotte, by the way," said
Charlotte. "And this is Mia."

"My name's Tilly," said Tilly. "I'd love to
work with you two, if you don't mind. My
friends on the team don't know how badly
I'm doing at science – or that I might not be
able to play. I really don't want to let them
down. They're counting on me."

Mia nodded sympathetically. She understood how Tilly felt – she didn't want to let down Princess Luna, either. "We've got to grant Tilly's wish," she whispered to Charlotte as they left the hall with Tilly. The Secret Princesses were depending on them to save the day!

CHAPTER FOUR
Bubble Trouble

Mia and Charlotte followed Tilly and her classmates down a corridor decorated with artwork. On one side the walls were hung with pretty daffodils made from scrunched-up pieces of bright yellow tissue paper, while painted scenes from fairy tales hung on the other side.

"That's lovely," said Mia, stopping in

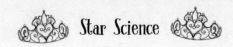

front of a picture of Cinderella's glass slipper. It was decorated with loads of glitter and reminded her of the sparkly slippers she and Charlotte wore at Wishing Star Palace.

"Hey, Tilly," said Charlotte. "Why is Cinderella rubbish at football?"

Tilly shrugged. "I don't know. Why?"

"Because she always runs away from the ball," said Charlotte.

A huge grin lit up Tilly's face. "Ha!" she laughed. "That's a good one! I'll have to tell it to the other girls on my team."

Mia gave Charlotte's hand a squeeze, proud that the joke had cheered Tilly up.

Tilly's class trooped into a dark classroom with pop music blasting out of it.

"Here you go," said the teacher, handing each student a glow stick.

Charlotte bent her glow stick. *SNAP!* It started to glow hot pink.

"Whoo hoo!" cried Mia, dancing around with a neon yellow glow stick.

Charlotte circled her arm around, making bright pink circles in the dark. Tilly threw her orange glow stick up in the air and caught it.

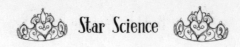

The classroom was soon lit up with flashes of hot pink, bright yellow, lime green and fluorescent orange as Tilly's classmates waved glow sticks in the dark and danced along to the music. It seemed more like a disco than a science lesson!

When the song finished, the teacher switched on the lights, making everyone blink. "Does anyone know how glow sticks work?" she asked.

"Magic, Mrs Dixon?" guessed the girl wearing cool pink trainers.

"No," chuckled Mrs Dixon. "It's a chemical reaction. Snapping a glow stick releases two different chemicals. When they combine, they glow." The teacher put

on safety goggles and poured clear liquid
from one beaker into a bowl. Then she
poured a different clear liquid into the bowl.
Suddenly, the clear liquid swirled with purple
neon light!

"Wow!" gasped the children as the teacher
held the bowl up to show them.

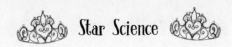

"Can I have a volunteer to come up here and try it?" asked the teacher.

"Put your hand up, Tilly," whispered Charlotte. "I'm sure you can do it."

"I don't know ..." said Tilly.

"Go for it," urged Mia. She was sure

Tilly could be good at science – they just needed to boost her confidence.

Tilly raised her hand tentatively.

"Ah, Tilly," said Mrs Dixon. "Thank you for volunteering. Come on up here."

The teacher handed Tilly a pair of safety goggles and she put them on. "Mix the two liquids together."

Tilly poured one liquid into a bowl. She picked up the second beaker and poured it into the bowl.

"She's doing fine," Mia whispered to Charlotte.

Then, with trembling hands, Tilly picked up the bowl. The liquid sloshed around, starting to glow with violet-coloured light. *SPLASH!* The bowl slipped out of Tilly's hands and fluorescent purple liquid spilled all over the teacher's desk!

"Oops! Never mind," said Mrs Dixon kindly, mopping up the neon-coloured spill.

Tilly pulled off the goggles, her cheeks red with embarrassment. "I told you I'm hopeless at science," she said, returning to Mia and Charlotte. "I get so nervous. I just can't stop thinking about what will happen if I don't improve my grade."

"It was an accident," said Mia. "Don't worry. There are lots of experiments to try.

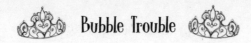

You'll get a gold star – promise!"

A bell rang, telling the children it was time to change classrooms. The next classroom Tilly's class visited was bright and sunny. There were small pots of cress growing on the windowsills.

Mr Watson, the teacher who had made the fizzy fountain in assembly, had a cute little voice-activated robot and was showing the children what it could do. The robot was white, with red lights shining from its eyes. It had wheels instead of feet and was only as tall as the teacher's knee.

"Bring me a book," said the teacher. The robot glided over to the bookshelf, picked up a book and wheeled back to the teacher.

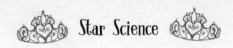

"That's so cool!" said Charlotte.

"Too bad the robot can't do science experiments for me," said Tilly.

There was a knock on the door and the headteacher came into the classroom.

"Good morning, Mrs Cooper!" chorused the children, standing up.

"Children, we have an important visitor today," said Mrs Cooper. "A school inspector has come to observe our Science Day."

A tall woman stepped into the classroom, wearing a green suit with an official-looking badge around her neck. She had long dark hair with an ice-blonde streak and her glittering green eyes were fixed on Tilly. It wasn't an inspector – it was Princess Poison!

As the pupils took turns giving the robot commands, Princess Poison strolled over to Mia and Charlotte. "How are you enjoying Science Day, girls?" she asked them, smirking.

"I was enjoying it a lot more before you turned up," Charlotte retorted.

"Tut, tut, tut," said Princess Poison, with a mean smirk.

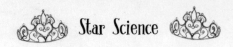

"That's no way to speak to your elders, especially at school. I guess it's time to teach you a lesson."

She opened her briefcase and took out her magic wand. Pointing it at the little robot, she said:

> "To be powerful is what I demand.
> Make that robot obey my every command!"

Green magic flowed from her wand to the robot, just as Tilly was having her turn.

"Pick up my pencil," Tilly ordered the robot.

"Pinch that girl," Princess Poison commanded at the same time.

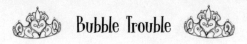

The robot's eyes changed from red to green. It reached out stiffly and pinched Tilly's arm.

"Ouch!" cried Tilly, rubbing her arm.

Princess Poison chortled gleefully. "Oh yes," she said. "I like my new toy. I'm going to call her EVA. That's short for Extra Villainous Assistant!"

As she returned to her desk and picked up

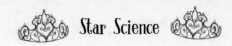

her pencil, Tilly sighed. "I couldn't even get that robot to follow my orders."

"That wasn't your fault," said Mia. But before she could explain, a bell rang. It was time for Tilly's class to move on again.

In the next classroom, the teacher, Mrs Khan, had set up plastic trays filled with soapy water around the classroom. She dipped a plastic wand in one of the trays and blew on it. A bubble floated in the air, a rainbow shimmering on its surface.

"When you mix washing-up liquid and water, the soap forms a very thin wall and traps air inside," explained Mrs Khan.

The bubble drifted down and landed on her desk. *POP!*

"But bubbles are very fragile," said Mrs Khan. "So try adding different things to the bubble mixture to see what makes them bigger and stronger." She showed the children the materials they could use – sugar, lemon, fruit juice, syrup, vinegar and salt.

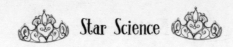
One group tried adding vinegar to their bubble mixture. "Yuck!" said the red-haired girl with the polka-dotted hair bow. "That stinks!" The vinegar didn't make the bubbles any bigger and they still popped just as easily as the normal bubbles.

"Let's see what this does," said Mia, handing Tilly the syrup bottle.

Tilly poured a small amount of syrup into her water tray and swirled it around. Dipping the plastic wand into the mixture, she blew an enormous bubble. It hovered in the air and didn't pop when Tilly gave it a nudge.

"Wow!" said Tilly. "That works really well! I can't wait to show Mrs Khan! Maybe I'll get a gold star!"

But before Tilly could get the teacher's attention, EVA glided into the classroom. The robot jabbed Tilly's bubble roughly.

POP!

Mia wheeled around and saw Princess Poison watching them from the doorway.

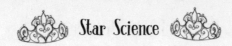

She gave them a little wave then clicked her
fingers to summon EVA back to her.

Tilly looked crestfallen.

"We can't let Princess Poison get away
with this," said Mia. "We've got to show
Tilly that she CAN be good at science."

"Are you thinking what I'm thinking?"
Charlotte asked, holding up her pendant.

Mia nodded. It was time to make a wish!

CHAPTER FIVE
Slime Time

Mia and Charlotte held their glowing pendants together, forming a heart. "I wish for Tilly to make amazing bubbles," whispered Mia.

There was a flash of golden light and an enormous, beautiful iridescent bubble rose out of Tilly's water tray. Then another even bigger bubble floated out of the tray.

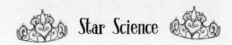

More and more magical bubbles rose into the air. Soon, the classroom was filled with gigantic bubbles, shimmering with all the different colours of the rainbow.

"Look!" shouted the girl with the hair bow. "Tilly's made huge bubbles!"

"Oh my gosh," cried the girl with the pink trainers. "They're bigger than my head!"

Boys and girls jumped around the classroom, batting the bubbles around and trying to pop them.

"Yippee!" cried Tilly, leaping up and tapping one of the bubbles with her hand.

"Well done, Tilly," said Mrs Khan, coming back into the classroom. "You get a gold star for working out that adding syrup to

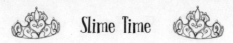

the mixture makes big, strong bubbles." She added a gold star to a chart that had the names of all of the children in Tilly's class.

Tilly beamed at the teacher's praise. Mia grinned at Charlotte.

The bell rang for playtime. Tilly's classmates grabbed their coats off pegs in the corridor and ran out into the playground.

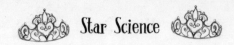
Tilly lagged behind, so she could speak to
Mia and Charlotte alone.

"How did you do that?" she asked them,
her eyes wide.

"Magic!" Mia told her.

"We're training to become Secret
Princesses," Charlotte explained to her.

Slime Time

"We're here to make your wish come true –
to help you get a good grade in science."

"Is this another joke?" Tilly asked
Charlotte.

"I promise we aren't joking," said Mia.
"Secret Princesses grant wishes using magic.
We're still in training, but our necklaces let
us make three small wishes."

"That's … amazing," said Tilly, her brown
eyes growing wider with astonishment.

"It is amazing," agreed Charlotte. "And
it's also a secret. You mustn't tell anyone else
about the magic."

Tilly pretended to zip up her mouth.

"It's playtime, girls," Mrs Khan said,
looking up from the tests she was marking.

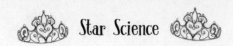

"Go outside and get some fresh air."

Tilly led Mia and Charlotte out to the playground. A group of girls were sitting by the side of a grassy field. They waved at Tilly.

"Those are the girls on my football team," said Tilly.

Mia and Charlotte followed Tilly across the playground to her friends.

"Hey, Tilly," said a girl with her hair in a bun. "Will you sit next to me on the minibus when we go to the football tournament?"

"Sure, Claudia," said Tilly.

"The team from Oakfield School is supposed to be really good," said a girl who was sitting on a football.

"Yeah, but we've got Tilly," said Claudia, putting her arm around Tilly's shoulder. "She'll score lots of goals for us."

Tilly smiled nervously. "I hope so …"

"I'm going to wear ribbons to match our school colours," said the girl with the pink trainers, who was plaiting her blonde hair.

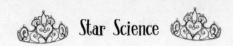

"Oh, good idea, Francesca," said Tilly. "Let's all do that!"

"My mum said that you can all come to my house after the tournament," said Francesca. All the girls shrieked excitedly, except for Tilly, who looked miserable at the thought of missing all the fun.

"Um, should we play?" Tilly asked. "We need all the practice we can get."

"Good thinking," said the girl on the football, getting to her feet.

"Want to play with us?" Tilly asked Mia and Charlotte.

Mia and Charlotte exchanged looks. Mia knew her sporty friend would probably love to join in, but Mia wasn't keen on football.

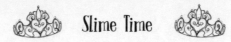

"No thanks," said Charlotte loyally. "We'll just cheer you on."

Tilly's friends ran on to the playing field and challenged a group of boys kicking a football to a game. Tilly soon took control of the ball and kicked it down the grassy field, dodging past the boys' defence. It was obvious, even to Mia, that Tilly was really good.

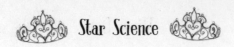

"Go, Tilly!" Mia cheered.

"Tilly – pass the ball to Francesca," Claudia shouted.

Thwack! Tilly passed the ball to her teammate, then sprinted forward. Francesca kicked the ball and it soared high in the air.

"Head it, Tilly!" yelled Claudia.

Tilly jumped into the air and hit the ball with her forehead. It flew to the back of the net – *SWISH!* – scoring a goal for the girls' team.

"Yay!" cheered Mia and Charlotte as Tilly's teammates ran over to hug her. Claudia, the team captain, gave her a high five.

"When Tilly's playing football, she doesn't get nervous or have any trouble

concentrating," Charlotte said thoughtfully.

Mia nodded. "She's totally focussed on the game."

The bell rang to say playtime was over. Tilly jogged over to Mia and Charlotte, her cheeks flushed pink from running around.

"You're really good at football, Tilly," Charlotte said.

"Thanks," said Tilly.

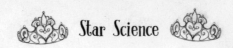

"But I'm not going to be able to help my friends at the tournament if I don't get a good grade today."

"You've got one gold star already," Mia reminded her. "I'm sure you can get more."

"I'll try my best," said Tilly. "I know the other girls are counting on me." She led them to a classroom that said "Miss Powell" on the door.

"This is my classroom," said Tilly, going inside.

A dark-haired teacher in a suit was holding a big blob of glittering green slime. She pulled her hands apart and the slime stretched out, gooey and stringy.

"It looks like snot!" whispered Charlotte.

"Have a go making your own slime," said Miss Powell. "There are instructions and ingredients on each table."

Tilly went over to a table. "OK," she said, rolling up her sleeves. "This time I'm going to be really careful."

"Just concentrate on what you're doing, the way you do when you're playing football," said Charlotte.

"You'll be fine," said Mia, "as long as you focus on following the instructions."

Tilly measured out a spoonful of washing powder and mixed it with water in a bowl. Then she squeezed sticky white glue into the mixture and swished it around with her hands.

"You're doing great," said Charlotte.

"It doesn't look right," said Tilly, frowning.

"Don't panic," said Mia calmly.

"Oh!" said Tilly. "I need to add food colouring."

PLIP! PLOP! She added a few drops of green food colouring to the mixture and kneaded it together. It was starting to look right!

"Don't forget this," said Charlotte, holding up a tube of silver glitter.

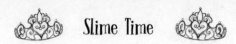

Tilly shook some glitter into the green goo, making it sparkle.

"Can I feel it?" asked Mia. She plunged her hands into the slime. *SQUELCH!*

"Ew!" she squealed, giggling. "That's so gross!"

"Good work, Tilly," said Miss Powell, coming around to check the children's work. "When you mix glue and washing powder, the particles link together, making a strong chain. That's why it's so stretchy and slimy."

There was a knock on the door and Princess Poison stepped into the classroom. EVA glided next to her, carrying her mistress's briefcase.

"Speaking of slimy ..." groaned Charlotte.

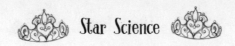
"Hello," said Princess Poison, flashing her badge at Miss Powell. "I'm inspecting the school today. May I have a word with some of your pupils?" Pointing at Tilly, Mia and Charlotte, she said, "Perhaps these three little girls?"

"Of course," said Miss Powell. "Girls, be on your best behaviour for our visitor. The rest of you, come to the canteen for lunch."

"Now what have we here?" said Princess Poison, once they were alone in the classroom. She stuck a fingernail in Tilly's slime, then flicked it at Mia and Charlotte. "It doesn't look right to me. We need to test it." Turning to the robot, she said, "EVA – throw the slime against the wall."

The robot obeyed Princess Poison's order.
It flung all of Tilly's carefully made slime
across the classroom.

SPLAT! Gooey green slime dripped down
the whiteboard.

"Oh no," wailed Tilly. "Now I won't get a

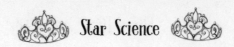
gold star for my slime! And I'm going to get in big trouble for making a mess."

"No, you're not," said Charlotte angrily. "She isn't really a school inspector. Her name is Princess Poison and she's trying to spoil your wish."

"But we aren't going to let her," said Mia.

"We'll see about that," said Princess Poison. "Wand!" she called, clicking her fingers. The robot took Princess Poison's wand out of her briefcase and wheeled it over to her. Pointing her wand at the slime, Princess Poison hissed a spell:

**I'll spoil Tilly's wish in
double-quick time,
By covering her classroom in
gooey green slime!**

There was a flash of green light and suddenly the whole classroom was splattered in slime. Green goo dripped from the lights, covered the desks and pooled in puddles on the floor. Tilly, Mia and Charlotte were completely drenched in slime, too!

"Yuck!" said Mia, grabbing some tissues and wiping slime off her face.

"You children have been very naughty." Princess Poison shook her finger at them.

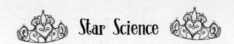

"Come along, EVA," she said. The little robot followed her, its wheels skidding on the slime on the way out of the classroom.

"Miss Powell's going to think I made this mess," said Tilly, slime dripping from her hair. "I'll probably get a detention and be kicked off the football team for good!"

"No you won't," said Mia. "Because we're going to make another wish!"

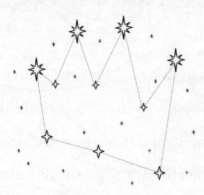

CHAPTER SIX
Classroom Catastrophe

Mia and Charlotte held their pendants together. "I wish for Tilly's classroom to look lovely," said Charlotte.

"And for us to be tidied up, too!" Mia quickly added.

Magical light shot out of the heart and every trace of slimy green goo vanished, except for the slime the children had made.

All of the workstations had been tidied up and the whiteboard gleamed. There was now a cosy reading corner with comfy beanbags, an aquarium with colourful tropical fish swimming around it, and a display with glittering crystals and posters about the night sky.

"Phew!" said Charlotte. "Thank goodness we don't look like swamp monsters any more!"

Miss Powell came back to her classroom, holding a stack of maths books.

"Thanks so much for tidying up, girls," she said, dropping the books down on her desk. "Tilly, I'm giving you a gold star for your excellent slime, and another one for cleaning

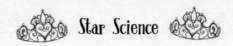
up the classroom." She stuck another two stars on the chart next to the one Tilly had earned for her bubbles.

"Thanks, Miss Powell," Tilly said, beaming with pride.

"Now go and get some lunch." The teacher winked at them. "I hear there's apple crumble and custard for dessert."

"Why didn't Miss Powell notice that her classroom looked different?" asked Tilly as they hurried to the canteen.

"That's all part of the magic," explained Charlotte.

Tilly showed them where to get a tray and they stood in the lunch queue. As they waited, Mia's tummy rumbled loudly.

"Science is hungry work," teased Charlotte.

"I'm starving too," said Tilly.

When they'd got their food, Charlotte asked, "So is Science Day more fun than you thought it would be, Tilly?"

"Yes," admitted Tilly. "The experiments are pretty cool. And I can do them properly if I concentrate." She pushed pasta around her plate. "But I'm still worried about my science project. My volcano still isn't finished. I messed up and had to start again so I'm behind the rest of the class. If my volcano doesn't work, my science grade won't be good enough for me to be allowed to play in the tournament."

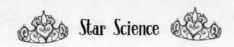
"We'll help you finish it," said Mia. "I love making things."

Charlotte nodded. "You can work on it in the lunch break."

Two of the girls from Tilly's football team came over to their table, holding trays with empty plates.

"Meet us on the field when you've finished eating?" asked Claudia.

"I'm sorry, guys," Tilly said, sighing. "I can't play after lunch. I need to finish my science project."

"No worries," said Francesca. "We'll miss you though."

"Good luck finishing your project," said Claudia, waving as she and Francesca

headed out to the playground.

"They seem really nice," said Mia.

"They are," agreed Tilly. "They're my best friends. I can't let them down!"

"You won't!" said Charlotte. "So let's eat up. Then we can get your project done and you can play with them on Saturday."

They quickly gulped down their lunches.

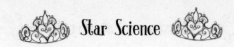
"Yum," said Charlotte, scooping up the last bite of her apple crumble. "Custard's my favourite."

After putting away their trays, the girls headed back to Tilly's classroom. The volcano projects were resting on windowsills around the classroom.

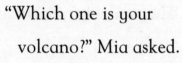

"Which one is your volcano?" Mia asked.

"The most rubbish one," said Tilly, picking up a rather lopsided papier-mâché volcano covered in long strips of newspaper.

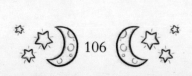

Unlike her classmates' volcanoes, Tilly's one wasn't painted yet. She glanced up at the clock on the wall and sighed. "I'm never going to get it done in time."

"When you're playing football, do you ever give up trying to score a goal before the game is over?" Charlotte asked Tilly.

"Of course not," said Tilly.

"Well then," said Charlotte. "Pretend this is the last ten minutes of an important match. You need to finish your volcano before the referee blows the whistle."

Tilly put on an apron, a determined look on her face. "I'm going to score a goal! I mean, finish my project!" She went over to the sink and took down some paints.

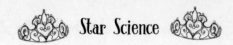
As Tilly painted the base of her volcano green and brown, Mia wandered over to the science display. There was a poster showing all the planets in the solar system, and glow-in-the-dark stars arranged in the shape of the Big Dipper. It reminded Mia of the tiara constellation and their friends at Wishing Star Palace.

"Are you thinking about Princess Luna too?" Charlotte murmured.

Mia nodded. "If we don't grant Tilly's wish, Luna might lose her magic for ever," she said, feeling a lump in her throat at the terrible thought.

"But we are going to grant Tilly's wish," said Charlotte. She looked over at Tilly, who

was adding red paint to look like flowing lava. "Tilly's working hard on her volcano. She'll get a good grade for it as long as the experiment works."

"But what about Princess Poison?" worried Mia. "She won't stop doing mean things. And what if Hex turns up?" Hex was Princess Poison's nasty assistant.

"Whatever she tries, we can handle it," said Charlotte confidently. "After all, we still have one wish left."

Mia looked down at her necklace. The pendant was glowing very faintly, because there was only a little magic left. She and Charlotte would have to choose their last wish very, very carefully.

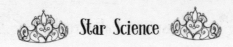

"Hey, guys," called Tilly. "What do you think?"

Mia and Charlotte went over to check out her volcano.

"It's looking good," said Mia.

"You're nearly done!" Charlotte added.

"What should I do now?" Tilly asked. "I want to make it even better."

"How about doing a fact sheet about volcanoes to go with it?" suggested Mia.

"Good idea," said Tilly.

Tilly went over to the book corner and found some books about volcanoes. They all flipped through them.

"The hot rocks inside a volcano are called magma," said Tilly, writing out the fact neatly.

"Some volcanoes are under the ocean floor," Mia read aloud.

"Wow," said Charlotte. "Volcanic eruptions can blast rocks as far as thirty kilometres into the atmosphere!"

"I just hope my volcano does erupt," said Tilly, quickly writing down the facts.

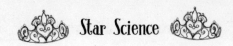

The girls were so busy helping Tilly research volcano facts that nobody heard Princess Poison enter the classroom with EVA at her side.

"Oh, can I help too?" she asked. She tapped her lips with her index finger, pretending to think. "I think it could use some more green." She turned to the robot. "EVA, turn the volcano green."

Wheeling over, the robot picked up the bottle of green paint and raised it over Tilly's volcano, about to pour it on top.

"No!" cried Tilly in alarm.

"Oh no you don't," said Mia, snatching the bottle. Paint splashed on EVA, covering the robot with green splodges.

"Silly girl, you can't stop me," said Princess Poison, her eyes glinting nastily. "Destroy that volcano!" she ordered the robot, putting her hands on her hips.

"Quick! Make a wall!" shouted Charlotte. Tilly, Mia and Charlotte stood side by side, protecting Tilly's volcano from the robot.

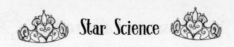
The robot tried to get around them but the girls linked arms and shuffled over to block its way.

"COMMAND FAILED," said EVA, spinning round and round in circles. "ERROR REPORTED."

"Stupid hunk of metal," growled Princess Poison. She kicked at EVA but the robot moved just in time. Turning to Tilly, her eyes narrowed menacingly, Princess Poison gave a long, horrible laugh.

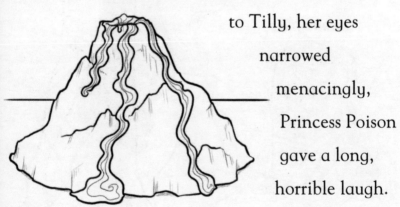

"Didn't I just hear you say you want your volcano to erupt? Well, let me help you out." She took out her wand and spat out a terrible curse:

**Magic, make this
volcano blow,
So red-hot lava
starts to flow!**

Green magic
flew out of Princess
Poison's wand,

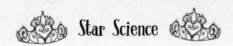
sending out a shower of green sparks on to Tilly's volcano.

The classroom started to rumble and shake. Books fell off the bookshelves and artwork fluttered down from the walls. Thick grey smoke started puffing out of Tilly's volcano and the classroom suddenly got so hot it felt like they were inside an oven.

"Looks like things are hotting up in here!" said Princess Poison. Fanning herself, she left the classroom, with EVA wheeling obediently behind her.

Tilly covered her mouth, coughing as stinky, black smoke billowed out of the volcano and filled the classroom.

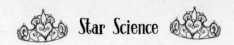

"Quick, Charlotte, we've got to do something!" cried Mia. "The volcano's going to explode!"

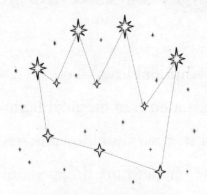

CHAPTER SEVEN

Dr Potions

Fighting their way through the clouds of smoke, Mia and Charlotte joined their necklaces together. The pendants were glowing so faintly that they could barely see them through the thick smoke. The heat made Mia feel like she was melting.

"I wish for Tilly's volcano to go back to the way it was before!" Charlotte shouted

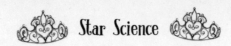

over the noisy rumbling.

There was a flash of magical light and everything stopped shaking. The smoke cleared, the temperature dropped and Tilly's volcano was once again just made of paper and glue.

"Phew!" said Charlotte, wiping sweat off her forehead. "Talk about being in the hot seat."

Tilly managed a small smile, but Mia could tell that she was frightened by what Princess Poison had done. Her hands were shaking as she finished writing out her volcano facts.

"I can't believe Princess Poison actually tried to blow up Tilly's volcano," Mia said.

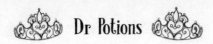
"I can," said Charlotte grimly. "She'll do anything if it means hurting the Secret Princesses."

Mia glanced down at her necklace nervously. They had used up all their magic, so if Princess Poison tried anything else to spoil Tilly's wish it would be very hard to stop her.

The bell rang and the lunch break was over. Tilly's classmates trooped back indoors, all their cheeks pink and their hair messy from playing outside.

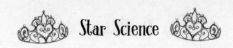

"Did you finish your volcano?" Claudia asked Tilly.

"Yes," said Tilly, taking her paintbrushes over to the sink to clean them.

"It looks really good," said Francesca.

"Thanks," said Tilly nervously. "I just hope it works."

"Form an orderly line, everyone," Miss Powell instructed her class. "A guest speaker is teaching us about electricity this afternoon."

Mia and Charlotte joined the back of the line behind Tilly. The class followed Miss Powell into the hall. They sat down at the back, next to a box filled with footballs, plastic cones and other PE equipment.

Glancing at the footballs nervously, Tilly said, "If my volcano doesn't work, my grade still won't be good enough for me to play in the tournament this weekend."

"Your volcano is great," Mia reassured her.

"Really?" asked Tilly.

"Definitely," said Charlotte.

"Boys and girls," said the headmistress, "It is my pleasure to introduce our special guest scientist, Dr Potions!"

A short, tubby man in a white coat

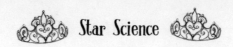

stood by her side.

Mia gasped. Dr Potions was actually Hex – Princess Poison's nasty assistant! "We've got to tell somebody," she whispered to Charlotte. "I'm sure he's going to do something bad."

Charlotte waved her hand in the air urgently, but Miss Powell shook her head. "Save your questions for after the presentation," she told Charlotte.

"Hello, young scientists," said Hex, holding up two lemons. "I am going to show you how to make a battery out of lemons." He clipped a wire on to each lemon. "Eureka!" he said, attaching the other ends of the wires to a lightbulb. But nothing happened.

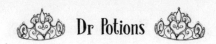

The lightbulb didn't turn on.

"OK, forget that," said Hex, tossing
the lemons aside. "Let's make some static
electricity instead." He pulled out a balloon
and rubbed it vigorously against his hair.

POP! The balloon burst, startling Hex.

"Yikes!" he said, jumping into the air.

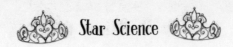

The children giggled, but Mia noticed someone in the hall who wasn't amused – Princess Poison had her hands on her hips and looked furious.

"This guy is worse at science than me," Tilly whispered to Mia and Charlotte.

"It's because he's—" Mia started to explain, but Miss Powell turned to them with her finger on her lips.

Next, Hex took out a glass globe with brightly coloured beams of light dancing around inside it. It looked like a thunderstorm raging inside a glass ball.

"How is it doing that?" Claudia called out.

"Um, it's magic," said Hex.

"Actually," said Miss Powell, "it's called

a plasma ball. There's gas and electricity inside it."

"Ha ha. That's right," said Hex. "I was just testing you." He laughed nervously as Princess Poison glared at him.

"Er, for this next experiment," said Hex, "I need a volunteer."

Lots of children raised their hands. Tilly's hand shot into the air too.

"What are you doing?" Charlotte whispered.

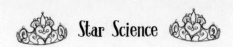
"I want to show Miss Powell that I'm good at science now," said Tilly.

"I don't think that's—" Mia started, but Hex interrupted her.

"You!" said Hex, pointing straight at Tilly. "Come up here, please."

"Uh oh," said Charlotte.

"Don't go!" said Mia.

"It's OK," said Tilly confidently. "I know I can do it if I concentrate." She made her way to the front of the hall.

"Place your hand on top of the plasma ball," Hex instructed her.

Tilly put her hand on the glass globe. The pink and purple light swirling around inside of it leaped towards her fingertips.

"Oooh," gasped the children.

"It looks like your little friend is quite the scientist now," Princess Poison hissed, sneaking up behind the girls with EVA.

"No thanks to you," said Charlotte.

"You girls get an A+ for effort," said Princess Poison. "But sadly you're going to fail at granting Tilly's wish."

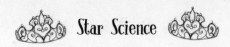

"No we aren't," said Mia. "Tilly likes science now, and her project turned out brilliantly."

"But you're forgetting something, Miss Smartypants," said Princess Poison, tapping Mia's head with a sharp fingernail. "You don't have any wishes left!"

At the front of the hall, Tilly was moving her hands over the plasma ball, making the electricity inside it leap and dance around.

"I think Tilly's in for a shock," said Princess Poison. "A very big shock."

Pointing her wand at the plasma ball, Princess Poison uttered a spell:

The tiara star wishes I will block,
So give that girl an electric shock!

"We've got to stop her!" gasped Mia.

Thinking fast, Charlotte grabbed a football from the box of PE equipment. She flung the ball in the air. It sailed over the children sitting on the floor, arcing towards the front of the hall. "Tilly!" she shouted. "Head the ball!"

Tilly reacted instantly – her reflexes as quick as the

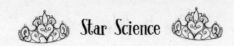

lightning inside the plasma ball. She jumped in the air and hit the ball with her head, just as green light shot out of Princess Poison's wand.

WHUMP! The football hit the magical green light, sending it flying back in the opposite direction.

ZAP! The green light sizzled Princess Poison with an electric shock!

"Owwww!" shrieked Princess Poison. Her hair frizzed out wildly around her head.

"And that concludes our lesson on electricity," Hex said hastily, rushing over to help Princess Poison.

"You idiot!" screeched Princess Poison, grabbing Hex.

ZAP! Her hands gave Hex an electric shock, making his hair stand up on end as well!

"Yay!" cheered the children, thinking it was all part of the presentation.

"We're done here," said Princess Poison, dragging Hex out of the hall with EVA gliding along after them.

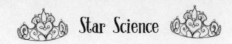

As they left, Charlotte grinned at Mia. "Now that really is shocking!"

CHAPTER EIGHT
Star Scientist

"Well done," said Miss Powell, when Tilly returned to her classmates. "You deserve another gold star for helping Dr Potions."

Tilly smiled as Claudia and Francesca clapped her on the back.

"Settle down, everyone," said Miss Powell. "Now, back to our classroom. We're going to try out our volcanoes."

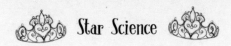

The boys and girls filed out of the hall obediently. As they walked down the corridor, Tilly whispered, "What really happened in the hall? Why did Charlotte throw me the football?"

"Dr Potions really works for Princess Poison," Mia whispered back. "His real name is Hex."

"They were trying to give you an electric shock," Charlotte explained in a low voice as they entered Tilly's classroom.

"But they got a shock instead," said Mia, "thanks to your brilliant football skills."

"Get your volcanoes out now, everyone," said Miss Powell. "Let's see if your projects have been successful."

Tilly went over to get her volcano and carried it back to her desk. The paint had dried while they had been in the hall. It looked pretty good!

Uncapping a marker pen, Miss Powell wrote instructions on the whiteboard:

1. *Place three tablespoons of bicarbonate of soda inside your volcano.*

2. *Add two drops of red food colouring.*

3. *Pour in vinegar and watch what happens!*

"Now for the moment of truth," said Tilly anxiously. "What if I mess it up?"

"It will be fine," said Mia.

"Just follow the instructions and pay attention," advised Charlotte. "Like when you're playing football."

Tilly carefully measured out three spoonfuls of bicarbonate of soda and added them to her volcano. Then – *plip! plop!* – she added the food colouring.

"Here goes," said Tilly, carefully pouring

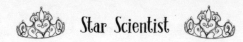

in the vinegar.

Mia held her breath. Would it work?

FIZZZZZ! Foamy red lava spewed out of Tilly's volcano and poured down the sides of her papier-mâché mountain.

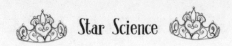
"Yay!" cried Tilly. "It worked!"

"Good job, Tilly," said Miss Powell. "The vinegar and bicarbonate of soda react together and release carbon dioxide."

"Just like Mr Watson's Fizzy Fountain," said Tilly.

"That's right," said Miss Powell, impressed. She took out her chart and added two gold stars – one for the volcano and one for helping Dr Potions – to the three Tilly had already earned. "You've been a Star Scientist today, Tilly. You showed excellent effort and tried lots of different experiments. Five gold stars means that your science grade is an A!" She jotted down Tilly's mark.

"Hurrah!" cheered Mia and Charlotte.

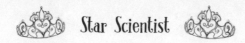

"I'm going to tell your coach that you can play in the tournament on Saturday," Miss Powell said. "I hope you girls win."

The teacher moved on to look at the other children's volcanoes.

"Thank you two so much," said Tilly, her brown eyes shining happily. "This was actually sort of fun!"

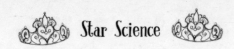

"That's OK," said Charlotte, smiling back at Tilly. "We had fun too."

"And my wish has come true," said Tilly. "I got a good grade in science so I can play in the tournament this weekend!"

Sparkly pink clouds suddenly puffed out of all the volcanoes in the classroom. Candyfloss-coloured clouds floated up in the air, joining together to form a fluffy pink heart. Mia and Charlotte grinned at each other. They knew the magic was because they had granted Tilly's wish!

A message magically appeared in swirly silver writing on the whiteboard. It said:

Use your shoes to come to the palace.

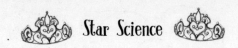

Glancing down, Mia saw that her ruby slippers had appeared on her feet. Charlotte was wearing hers, too.

The bell rang, announcing the end of the school day. All around the classroom, boys and girls shoved books and pencil cases into their schoolbags. Tucking their chairs under their desks, the children scrambled to collect their coats.

"Are you coming to football practice?" Claudia asked Tilly.

"Er, in a minute," said Tilly, putting her backpack on her shoulders.

"You should go with your friends," said Mia, giving her a hug. "We've got to go now."

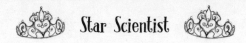

Hugging Mia close, Tilly whispered in her ear, "I'll never forget how you and Charlotte helped me. Thank you!"

"Good luck with your tournament," said Charlotte, giving Tilly a hug.

Waving goodbye, Tilly ran out to the playing fields with her friends.

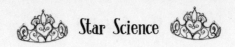

When the classroom was empty, Mia turned to Charlotte. "Ready?"

Holding hands, they clicked the heels of their slippers three times and called, "Wishing Star Palace!"

A moment later, they were back in the astronomy tower.

"Mia! Charlotte!" cried Princess Luna. "You two are such stars! Thank you so much for granting Tilly's wish!"

"Look through the telescope," said Alice.

Mia put her eye to the golden telescope and peered through the lens. Although Princess Poison's green mist still covered up most of the tiara constellation, one star was shining brightly in the night sky.

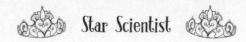

"Thanks to the wish you granted, that star is giving out magical light that will help keep Wishing Star Palace hidden," said Luna.

As Princess Luna pointed up at the sky, Mia noticed something on her wrist.

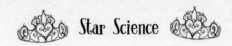
"Your bracelet!" she said. Unlike her wand, tiara and necklace, the gem on Luna's bangle was no longer green – it was back to being white.

Luna smiled as she glanced at her bracelet. "That reminds me," she said. "You deserve your first moonstones." Luna

touched her wand to Mia's pendant, but nothing happened. She shook her head. "Oops, I keep forgetting that my magic isn't working."

"Don't worry," said Alice, stepping in. She touched her wand to Mia's necklace and a pearly white moonstone suddenly appeared in the pendant. Then she tapped Charlotte's necklace, giving her a beautiful moonstone as well.

Luna sighed and fiddled with her moon-shaped pendant anxiously. "I feel so helpless not being able to grant the tiara star wishes."

"Mia and Charlotte have started breaking Princess Poison's curse," said Alice soothingly. "They'll soon grant the other three tiara star wishes and you'll get your magic back."

"We won't let anything stop us, Luna," promised Charlotte.

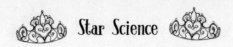

"Will you bring us back here when someone wishes on one of the other tiara stars?" asked Mia.

"Of course we will," said Luna.

"But you two should go home now," said Alice. "You need to get some rest."

"That reminds me of when you used to

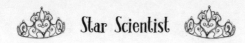

babysit for me," said Charlotte, grinning.
"You used to tell us to go to bed and get
some rest."

"Well, it's still true," said Alice, tweaking
one of Charlotte's curls. "Everyone needs
a good night's sleep – even pop stars and
trainee princesses!"

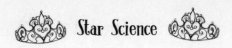

"Bye, Charlotte," said Mia, giving her best friend a hug.

"See you soon," said Charlotte.

Alice waved her wand and Mia felt herself soaring through a velvety black sky studded with twinkling stars.

The magic set Mia down in the park in the clothes she'd been wearing earlier. On her head was a bike helmet instead of a tiara. As she got back on her bike and cycled up the path, she saw Elsie on her pink bike, pedalling towards her on her own.

"Look, Mia!" cried Elsie. "I'm doing it! I'm riding my bike all by myself!"

"Go, Elsie!" cheered Mia, beaming at her little sister. "I knew you could do it!"

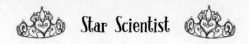

Just like I know that Charlotte and I will grant all the tiara star wishes, thought Mia. Because with lot of determination and a little help from your friends, you can do anything!

The End

Join Charlotte and Mia in their
next Secret Princesses adventure,
Sleepover School!

Read on for a sneak peek!

Sleepover School

"Pillow fight!" shouted Charlotte Williams, bashing her little brother Liam lightly on the head with a fluffy pillow.

"Oh no you don't!" giggled Liam, grabbing another pillow off his bed and flinging it at his sister.

Charlotte ducked, but Liam's twin brother Harvey swung a pillow at her back.

"Pillow fight!" shouted Charlotte Williams, bashing her little brother Liam lightly on the head with a fluffy pillow.

"Oh no you don't!" giggled Liam, grabbing another pillow off his bed and flinging it at his sister.

Charlotte ducked, but Liam's twin brother Harvey swung a pillow at her back.

"Gotcha!" cried Harvey.

"Hey!" protested Charlotte, laughing. "Two against one isn't fair!"

"Oh yes it is!" cried Harvey, bouncing up and down on his bed. The duvet had rocket ships and stars on it, just like the one on Liam's bed. "You're bigger than us!"

"OK, then," said Charlotte, with a grin. "You asked for it!" She tossed a pillow across the room at the exact moment the boys' bedroom door opened.

BOP! The pillow hit their dad right on the face!

"Oops!" said Charlotte. "Sorry, Dad!"

"Good shot," said Dad, chuckling. He was wearing an apron and had a tea towel slung over his shoulder. Picking up the pillow, Dad put it back on Liam's bed. "You lot need to settle down. It's nearly bedtime."

"Is Mum back from work yet?" asked Harvey.

"She's running late this evening," said Dad. "But she said to give you a kiss goodnight from her."

Charlotte's mum worked hard but she loved her new job. It was the reason they had moved to California from England not long ago.

"Aww," whined Liam. "But Mum always reads us a bedtime story."

"I'll read to you when I've finished tidying up the kitchen," said Dad.

"That's ages!" Harvey complained.

"I can read you guys a story," Charlotte offered.

"Thanks, Charlotte," said Dad, winking. "Goodnight, boys." Dad kissed the tops of Liam and Harvey's heads, then headed back downstairs.

"OK, guys," said Charlotte. "What should we read tonight?" She went over to the bookcase and ran her finger along the books' colourful spines. "How about this one?" she suggested, pulling a collection of fairy tales off the bookshelf.

"Yuck," said Liam, wrinkling his nose. "Fairy tales are always about princesses."

"Ugh," said Harvey, sticking out his tongue. "We don't want to read about boring old princesses."

"Who says princesses are boring?" Charlotte asked them.

"Me!" Liam and Harvey cried together.

"What about a princess who's also an astronaut?" said Charlotte.

Liam laughed. "Princesses can't be astronauts."

"Yeah," scoffed Harvey. "Princesses are silly and drippy. Astronauts are cool and brave."

"That's not true!" Charlotte said. She had to bite her lip to stop herself from telling her brothers that she had a friend who was a princess AND an astronaut! Princess Luna was cool and brave – and not the slightest bit silly or drippy! But Charlotte couldn't tell Liam and Harvey any of this, because Princess Luna was a Secret Princess – and Charlotte had to keep the secret! Charlotte was one of the lucky few who knew about these special princesses who could grant wishes using magic. It was because Charlotte and her best friend Mia were training to become Secret Princesses, just like Luna!

"Earth to Charlotte!" said Harvey, waving his hand in front of Charlotte's face.

"Sorry," said Charlotte, snapping out of her daydream. "Why don't you two choose a book?"

Liam and Harvey searched through their bookcase.

"This one!" said Liam, pulling out a well-worn book. He handed Charlotte the copy of *Spaceman Sam Saves the Day.*

Charlotte stifled a groan. She'd read this book to her brothers so many times she practically knew the story by heart!

The twins cuddled up on Liam's bed as Charlotte read them the story about an astronaut who landed on a planet made of jelly.

"'Then Spaceman Sam got back into his rocket and blasted back to Earth. The End,'" read Charlotte, shutting the book's tattered cover.

Liam yawned and rubbed his eyes as Harvey climbed into his own bed.

As the twins snuggled under their duvets, Charlotte went over to the window. Gazing out, she saw the silvery moon shining in the sky. *I wonder when Mia and I will earn our next moonstone*, Charlotte thought. To get their moonstone bracelets, she and Mia needed to earn three more moonstones by granting three wishes.

Charlotte glanced down at the gold necklace she was wearing under her pyjama top. A pearly white moonstone was embedded in the half-heart pendant. Soft moonlight streamed into the room, making Charlotte's necklace look like it was glowing. When she drew the curtains, Charlotte gasped. Her necklace was still glowing – but from magic, not moonlight!

"Night night," said Charlotte, quickly tucking her brothers into bed.

She hurried down the hall to her own bedroom, which had posters of her favourite gymnasts and pop stars on the walls. The top of her chest of drawers was cluttered with trophies from softball tournaments and medals from gymnastics competitions, while a framed picture of her and Mia hugging stood on her bedside table. Even though her best friend lived far away in England, Charlotte was about to go on an adventure with her!

Her heart racing with excitement, Charlotte held her pendant in her hand and murmured, "I wish I could see Mia."

The light shining out of the pendant grew brighter and brighter, making Charlotte's trophies and medals sparkle. Swirling around Charlotte, the magical light swept her away from her bedroom.

She landed in the grounds of Wishing Star Palace. Her pyjamas had been replaced by a beautiful pink princess dress and her fluffy slippers had magically transformed into sparkling ruby slippers. Patting her head, Charlotte felt a diamond tiara resting on her brown curls. Only one star shone in the inky black sky. It was so dark Charlotte could barely make out the palace's four white turrets rising in the distance.

"Hi, Charlotte!"

Startled, Charlotte jumped. Peering through the gloom, she suddenly realised who the voice belonged to.

"Mia!" she cried, hugging her best friend.

"It's so dark I didn't see you arrive."

Mia tapped the sapphire ring on her finger and a light shone out of it, illuminating her long blonde hair and blue eyes. "There," she said, grinning. "That's better."

Mia was wearing a golden princess dress, but her tiara and ruby slippers were identical to Charlotte's.

"Good thinking," said Charlotte, tapping her own sapphire ring to make more light. The girls had recently earned their rings for completing the previous stage of their training. The rings warned them when danger was near, but also came in handy when they needed light.

"Who? Who?" came a voice in the dark.

"It's just us," said Charlotte loudly, shining her ring around to see who it was. "Mia and Charlotte."

"Who? Who?" the voice repeated.

"It's Mia and Charlotte!" the girls shouted together.

But once again the mysterious voice echoed in the dark …

"WHO? WHO?"

A group of Secret Princesses suddenly appeared in front of Charlotte and Mia. The glow from their magic sapphire rings surrounded them like a blue aura, lighting up the dark night. Like the girls, they wore beautiful dresses and tiaras – but the princesses also carried wands.

"Hi, girls," said Princess Ella, who had a short, dark bob and was holding a pair of binoculars. She had a pawprint symbol on her necklace, because back in the real world she was a vet.

"Were you calling to us?" asked Mia.

"Nope," said Princess Sylvie, shaking her bright red curls. She had a cupcake pendant on her necklace because her special talent was for baking.

"Has someone wished on another tiara star?" Charlotte asked hopefully.

The Tiara Constellation was a group of stars in the shape of a tiara. When it appeared in the sky, the Secret Princesses granted the first wish made on each of the four stars at the tiara's points. The powerful magic from these special wishes kept Wishing Star Palace hidden in the clouds for another year.

"Not yet," said Princess Ella. "We invited you here because we're going on a Night-time Nature Walk. We're hoping to see some nocturnal animals."

Read Sleepover School to find out what happens next!

Fun Science Experiments

Do you want to be a super scientist like Tilly? Here are a few messy but fun science experiments to try. Remember ask a grown-up for permission first!

Papier-mâché Volcano

Vinegar is an acid and it reacts with bicarbonate of soda, which is a base. When they combine, they create carbon dioxide which bubbles out.

You will need:

- A plastic drinks bottle (without lid)
- Newspaper
- PVA glue
- Water
- A bowl
- A large cardboard box
- Scissors
- Masking tape
- Paint and brushes
- Vinegar
- Bicarbonate of soda
- Red food colouring
- A funnel

Instructions:

1. Cut out the bottom of the cardboard box to make the base

2. Stick the bottom of the drinks bottle to the base with glue

3. Rip half the newspaper into 2cm-wide strips

4. In a bowl, create a thin mixture of PVA glue and water

5. Scrunch up the rest of the newspaper. Dip it in the glue mixture then stick the newspaper on to the base, around the bottom of the bottle

6. Build up the volcano using more scrunched-up newspaper

7. Cover the scrunched-up newspaper with masking tape, running from the top of the bottle to the base, to make a frame

8. Dip the strips of newspaper into the glue mixture. Place them on top of the masking tape frame

9. Keep adding strips of newspaper until the shape starts to look like a volcano

10. Leave to dry for at least 24 hours, then paint!

How to Make Your Volcano Erupt:

1. Using the funnel, add two or three tablespoons of bicarbonate of soda to the bottle in the centre of the volcano.

2. Next, add a couple of drops of red food colouring.

3. Finally add the vinegar! Kaboom!

Fizzy Fountain

This experiment causes a chemical reaction between the mints and the cola. Thousands of tiny bubbles are formed, taking up more space than just the liquid. That's why foam spurts out of the bottle. *Whoosh!*

You will need:

- 1 large bottle of diet cola
- 1 tube of chewy mints
- 1 piece of paper

Instructions:

1. Place the bottle on flat ground outside

2. Remove the mints from their packaging

3. Make a funnel with the piece of paper and put the mints in it

4. Remove the lid of the cola bottle

5. Tip the mints into the cola bottle, using the paper funnel

6. Stand back and watch your fizzy fountain shoot into the air!

Secret
PRINCESSES

What would you wish for?

Are you a Secret Princess?

Join the Secret Princesses Club at:

secretprincessesbooks.co.uk

Explore the magic of the
Secret Princesses and discover:

♥ Special competitions! ♥
♥ Exclusive content! ♥
♥ All the latest princess news! ♥